Itchybald Scratchet

The Tales Begin

by

Sue C. Medcalf

Published

by

Sable Publishing House

PO Box 107, Wellington TA21 1BD, Somerset,
UNITED KINGDOM

ISBN 978 1 906255 64 0

9 781906 255640

Itchybald Scratchet

The Tales Begin

Published by Sable Publishing House, October 2014
Cover design © Sable Publishing House
Illustrations: Nicole Poulsom – colepoul@gmail.com
Editor: Claire Pickering

*   *   *   *   *   *   *

About the Author

Sue C. Medcalf

 Born in Bedford (UK), the eldest of four, Sue left school with average exam results. Ever since, her passion has been her family and she now has two adult sons and eight wonderful grandchildren. Until now, her family and work has been too demanding to commit to writing a book.

Having finally put pen to paper, finding the experience rewarding and therapeutic, Sue is now involved in an ongoing writing project, capitalising on her interest and research into badgers and wildlife in general, along with their behaviour and habitat. Her intention is to encourage children of all ages to benefit, enjoy and learn from reading.

Her family moved from Bedford to Somerset in the nineteen nineties, thereby enriching her understanding and enjoyment of nature and the countryside. The conflict between the need for human development owing to the increase in population and wildlife has been motivational to her writing.

About the Illustrator

Nicole Poulsom

Born and raised in Durban, South Africa, the eldest of two, Nicole was raised in an animal-friendly home and always had some form of pet. They were usually cats or a dog, but have also included rats, mice, fish and the odd budgie. She even helped catch snakes for her younger brother's collection. Nicole loved drawing and painting from a young age, but lacked the confidence to use her talents until now.

Now living in the UK, Nicole is happily settled in Kent with her husband, cat and spaniel, who all immigrated from South Africa. Having developed a passion for British wildlife, she is delighted to be included in this amazing project about Itchybald Scratchet and his friends.

"It is a wonderful thought that people reading this series will enjoy the characters created by the author. I hope my interpretation of Itchy and his friends enhances the story and enjoyment when reading about their adventures."

*　　*　　*　　*　　*　　*　　*

DEDICATION

This publication is dedicated to my dear mother, Mavis Yvonne Martin (1935–2014), and also my family, who mean so much to me and whose love, support and encouragement made it possible.

The inspiration for writing is from my sister, Dawn, without whom the *Itchybald Scratchet* series wouldn't have started. Dawn had badgers in her back garden and didn't know what to do about them. I did some research on badgers and their way of life, which lead me to write the book. My sister and I share a similar humour and our badger conversations developed into an amusing story, resulting in this publication.

I would particularly like to thank Nicole Poulsom for producing all the sketches used in the story and Sable Publishing House for guidance and support through to production. Thanks also to Claire Pickering of Richmond Pickering Ltd for editing, valuable help and advice.

Special thanks go to Pauline Kidner of the Secret World Wildlife Rescue Centre in Highbridge, Somerset. They do a great job caring for wild animals in need. You can learn more by visiting their website <www.secretworld.org>.

None of this would have been possible without the help and support of my husband, Ian, my family, friends and neighbours, to whom I am indebted.

*   *   *   *   *   *   *

Itchybald Scratchet – The Tales Begin

Book ONE of his amazing adventures

It was dusk. The air was heavy and damp, with storm clouds gathering over a leaden sky as badger, Itchybald Scratchet – Itchy to his friends, was making his way back to his sett (a badger's home). Normally he would have gone out at night, but their food stores were running low, so on this occasion he had gone out in the early afternoon.

Leaves were falling from the trees, their once golden russet shades now brown. The branches looked bleak and nearly bare as they creaked in the gusty wind. Bracken, damp leaves and twigs had blown into heaps underfoot as Itchy stumbled along muttering to himself, his handsome black-and-white face set in a deep badger frown. He could feel that winter would soon be upon them and he had a lot to think about. What could he do with so many mouths to feed?

Itchy scurried along as fast as his badger bulk would allow, his fur damp and the sack of fruit heavy against his body.

Itchy with his sack of apples

He still had quite a way to go before he reached his sett and Matty, his wife, would be wondering where he was. Itchy had risked straying from his usual patch today, lured out of his comfort zone by the smell of windfall apples. He was fast regretting his decision, now tired from carrying his bag as he struggled onwards against the worsening elements.

Dark, stormy night clouds now drifted across the sky and it had started to sleet. Cold, icy particles were beating down onto Itchy's head as he continued to mutter to himself. If he hadn't gone for those apples he would be home and warm by now, curled up in his favourite chair with a bowl full of Matty's lovely hot worm stew inside him. The thought both irritated and comforted him equally.

Still, if he hadn't have gone he would never have found out about the threat to his home. He had bumped into Peter Pheasant, the postman, who had told him all about the plans for the new houses for the 'upples' – a combination of 'up' and 'people', an animal term for humans. Better to be warned, I suppose thought Itchy.

When Peter had first told him of the housing, Itchy had not wanted to believe it. His family had occupied this sett for over fifty years, but the thought of his home being destroyed had to be taken seriously.

His mind taken up with thoughts of disaster and hot worm stew waiting, Itchy didn't see the gaping hole in front of him. He slipped on the muddy ground, scattering the fruit and splattering his already tangled, matted coat as he plunged down and down, into darkness and icy water.

As he hit the bottom of the disused well, a searing pain shot through his ankle. He tried to make out where he was in the gloom. A circular brick wall seemed to surround him, but it was too slippery to gain any hold to pull himself out. Itchy struggled to bring his huge mass upright, but his wet fur kept dragging him down and there was no way he could climb out unaided.

His claws scratched against the sides as he desperately clawed for gaps in the bricks, splintering and breaking against the unforgiving surface. With the walls covered in green moss and slime, he was unable to gain any grip. The cold muddy water was icy against his coat as he lay there for what seemed like an eternity, his back paw now throbbing. He screamed for someone to help him, but his cries were lost in the quickening, howling wind and sleet.

Suddenly, Itchy could sense something in the dim glow of the pale moonlight at the top of the well. He looked up and could make out a large form in the darkness. Please don't let it be an upple, he thought, they would never help him. He had heard tales of them setting out to kill badgers – a cull they had called it. He cowered down further into the gloom, breathing heavily, waist-deep in cold water, hoping the presence was friendly.

Itchy stuck in the well

Two ears appeared first, round, grey and large, followed by two big round eyes, button bright. Then a long pink nose with extremely long whiskers came into view.

The creature was roughly the same height as Itchy but with a much rounder belly. He looked as if he enjoyed his food. He was covered in a soft greyish-brown down. It was the biggest creature Itchy had ever seen. Wary, he cowered further down into the well.

"Hellooo, hellooo, anyone down there?" called out the creature.

"Yes, yes," yelled Itchy, relieved the voice was not that of an upple. "I tripped and fell, can you help me?"

"You look a bit stuck," said the voice, all the time chewing on a large slice of pizza. Cheese and tomato covered his paws, his cheeks bulging as he spoke.

Norm looking down into the well

"I think I am," replied Itchy. "I fell down here and can't get out. I think I have hurt my paw. Can you help me?"

"Just so happens, I think I can," said the voice in the darkening night, still chewing.

Itchy watched as the huge creature turned around as if to leave and for an instant Itchy wondered if he was going to walk away and abandon him. Suddenly, there was a swooshing sound in the air as something heavy seemed to drop down into the well, narrowly missing Itchy's head. It was a tail, wide, ridged, thick, long and very strong.

"Hang on to my tail and I will try to pull you out," said the voice, now seeming further away.

Itchy could just make him out, straining to remain upright as the weight of his tail hung over the edge. Itchy wrapped his paws around the grey tail as best he could.

Itchy trying to climb Norm's tail

Try as he might, each time his wet fur dragged heavily and he slid downwards again and again. The tail was very slippery which wasn't helping and Itchy wasn't exactly the lightest of badgers. He was tired and couldn't remember how long he had been down there.

"Put my tail around your waist," called out the voice, "and I will try something different this time. We can't leave you down there."

Itchy wound the tail around him and hung on as tightly as he could as the creature made his way slowly from the edge. One small step at a time, he dragged Itchy free of the cold muddy water, puffing and panting as he did so. With a last tug, Itchy was free.

Exhausted, they both lay on the ground, equally filthy, heaving and panting as they tried to catch their breath, the cold night air making them gasp. The creature moved his massive bulk to stand up, slipping and sliding in the mud as he tried to regain his balance. He took out a large red handkerchief, almost the size of himself, and began to wipe the remains of the pizza away, also mopping his brow and nose, which was now shining from exertion and the colour of his handkerchief.

"How do you do?" said the creature, introducing himself. "My name is Enor, Enor Mouse. I'm very pleased to make your acquaintance. All my friends call me Norm for short."

"I can't thank you enough," said Itchy, still shaken from his fall and the climb to safety. "My name is Itchybald Scratchet, Itchy to my friends." He offered a muddy claw to shake hands and the oversized mouse wiped his paw on the red handkerchief before accepting the badger's handshake. "Would you like to accompany me back to my home for some tea?" asked Itchy. It seemed the least he could do and besides, his stomach was now rumbling, his foot was sore and he was very cold. "My wife, Matty, cooks a fine worm stew if you are interested?" he added.

"I would love to!" said Norm, wishing it was pizza and not worm stew.

The two friends, their heads bent down into the howling wind and sleet, made their weary way towards Itchy's home. Itchy leaned on his new friend's arm, limping heavily owing to his twisted paw.

Matty's fur sometimes stuck up in tufts, giving her a somewhat quizzical look as if she was pondering the answer to whatever she had been asked. Beautiful black eyes like gleaming jewels shone out of her perfectly formed, but smaller-than-average badger face. Matty groomed herself proudly daily, with Itchy sometimes helping, but no matter how thorough they were, it was still matted in places.

Matty had been busy all day. Her daily tasks cleaning her home took up most of her time. It was very important to Matty that her home was clean and tidy.

Their sett had six rooms in total, dug under a large shed at the bottom of a garden belonging to a big house near the woods. It had beautiful fields with lovely views of the countryside beyond. It was ideal for foraging, but you would have to look very closely to find it. They had lived in the sett for a few years now and most of their time was spent in the main living area, which was warm, welcoming and cosy.

Matty cleaning the sett

A fire was lit in the hearth, giving off a soft glow, with a pot of hot worm stew bubbling nicely on the top, its aroma wafting around the sett. Itchy's favourite tartan armchair and footstool were waiting for him, found in an abandoned skip on a night-time raid, along with the settee and rugs. The table was already laid with dinner for two.

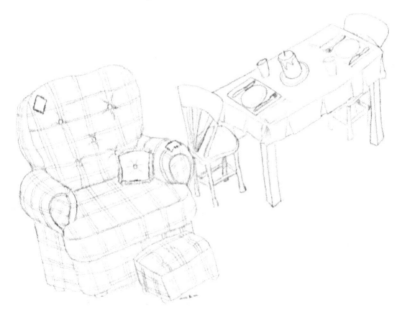

Itchy's armchair and table laid for dinner

Itchy's been gone a long time, thought Matty. Hopefully he will bring some nice fruit home with him. With the weather closing in, fruit would not be available for much longer and they would have to rely on bugs, berries and worms to survive the winter ahead. Where had he got to? The worm stew would spoil if he wasn't home soon, she thought, giving it another stir.

Plumping up the cushions, Matty suddenly heard voices on the wind and a kind of dragging sound, as if something was being pulled along the ground. As she went to look out of the doorway, leaves blew into the room. Peering into the darkness, she could see Itchy being helped along by a stranger, limping.

"Oh Itchy!" Matty cried. "What on earth have you been doing?"

"I fell down an old well," gasped Itchy in pain. "Fortunately for me this kind mouse, Norm, came along and rescued me. If it hadn't been for his strength, I don't think I would have got out. I have brought him home for some of your lovely stew as a reward, but I'm afraid I dropped the fruit, so we have no dessert for our guest."

"Never mind that!" exclaimed Matty as she rushed out to help Norm bring Itchy into the warm room.

A smell of worm stew welcomed them and they both lowered Itchy gently into his armchair. Matty pushed the footstool over for Itchy to rest his paw and began to rub him with a towel and groom him. Norm wiped his muddy paws before settling down in front of the roaring fire.

Later, after enjoyable worm stew, Itchy told them all about his conversation with Peter and how their home was under threat. If the upples built homes on the beautiful field near their sett, they would destroy the wood and all the countryside they loved so much, not to mention the other animals who were their friends. The woodland was abuzz with the news and the trio sat up late into the night discussing what to do.

The next day dawned bright, cold and dry after the previous night's storm; even the wind had died down. Itchy's foot, although sore, was better than it was and they felt happier in themselves as they had come up with a plan to save Badger Wood from the upples. Peter had informed them that there had been rumours about other housing developments moving to different locations following discoveries that the chosen site was of historical interest. All they had to do was to ensure that some artefacts were found to prevent the development from going ahead. They just had to find something old or valuable.

The trio wandered around the adjoining field later that day, digging sporadically, claws clogged with dirt. They stopped every now and again if they came across something of interest and each of them would come and look. There was the odd piece of glass from newish-looking beer bottles, a chipped plate – Matty recognised it as one she had seen in an upples's garden – and a shred of clothing from an old blue jumper Norm had seen the farmer wearing. But nothing was old enough to be of any use. Itchy even found an upple coin, which temporarily raised their hopes, but it turned out to be a recent one, just very dirty. All day they searched, but by dusk they still hadn't found anything so, weary and disheartened, they made their way back home.

The next day Matty had an idea. If there was nothing in the field at the moment to prevent the houses from being built, then maybe they could find some things and put them there. As long as the upples found something, it didn't really matter where it came from. After all, they weren't to know how it had got there. Then at least the field would be declared historic and so it could never be built on.

The only problem now was where they would find such things. It also meant they would need to leave their sett, journey beyond the field, beyond the wood and beyond the raging river. Further, even, than Great-Auntie Twiddle had been. But at least this way they would find old treasures to save their home. Great Auntie had left one really hard winter and had never been seen again. No one knew what had happened to her. Ever since, the Scratchets had stayed near their sett, too frightened to venture far, for fear of what might happen.

Two days later, Itchybald called a woodland meeting. The entire woodland had heard about the housing by this time, so everyone was there. Postman Peter the pheasant, rabbits, mice, Daphne the deer, and all manner of birds. Even the heron and the owl, Aubrey, were there, his feathers bristling and puffed up at being summoned. Creatures who were normally too busy for meetings, all concerned about their homes and the young, were all in attendance.

The woodland meeting

"I thought this area had been declared an area of outstanding natural beauty," said the owl, his head spinning indignantly, his tawny brown feathers blowing in the breeze, for generally he was very wise and thought he knew everything.

"So did I," said Daphne. The deer's beautiful, large brown eyes quickly filled with tears, her bottom lip quivering as she spoke, nervous in other people's company. "I have babies, too; I can't move them."

"It is a lovely place," said Itchy, "but the upples have decided they need extra space for houses and this seems a pleasant place for them to live. 'Nice views,' I heard one of the upples say."

The creatures broke out into a jumble of sound as the birds all tried to speak at once and the animals all tried to shout louder than the others to make their voices heard.

"Quiet!" shouted Itchy, now standing on a tree stump to make himself taller than the others. "Arguing amongst ourselves is not going to help. We all need to work together to try to save our homes. We have heard that if the field is to be saved it has to be declared a historic site, so let's make it one."

The muttering grew stronger as they all formed groups to discuss the implications of such a plan. How were they going to make it happen? Would it work and send the upples away?

"If you can all get some food together, whatever you can spare, Matty, Norm and I will travel faraway to gather what we need," said Itchy. "With winter nearly upon us we don't have a moment to lose. And we badgers are not good in the snow. We can't delay, for the upples will begin as soon as they can."

The animals began to disperse, muttering under their breath. What a worry, they all agreed, before scurrying off to check their winter food stores to see what they could give the trio to help with the journey, of which no one knew the destination or how long it would take.

By dusk the entire woodland was bustling. The moon cast eerie shadows through the dark branches as parcels of nuts, acorns, mushrooms, beetles and berries all wrapped in leaves arrived for Itchy, Matty and Norm to take with them.

The woodland animals bringing food parcels for the journey

As Norm was big and strong, his backpack was loaded with the most. Matty had a sack bag with her supplies in and Itchy had a heavy bag across his shoulder. If all went according to plan, they would eat some of the supplies on the journey, saving some for the return home, and the empty bags could be used to carry their goods in.

The three of them set off the following morning, the air damp but at least dry, albeit not as bright as they would have liked. It was a typical dull, grey autumn day. They wandered for what seemed like miles through damp leaves, until they came to a river. The water looked grey and uninviting, rushing currents pulling at the reeds and bulrushes on the riverbank. Matty looked at Itchy and Norm in horror.

"How on earth are we going to get across this river to the other side?" she said. "I don't like water."

"I don't know," said Norm. "We will have to think of something. I can't swim very well, either."

The three sat under the base of a tree eating berries while they discussed their next step.

"Perhaps we could swing across," said Norm, with a mouthful of blackberries. "Somehow ... maybe with branches or twine."

"No," said Itchy, "it's too risky; we might all fall in and drown. We will have to build a raft," he added. "Big and strong enough to take all of us down the river. We can go to a small village I have heard about. They might have what we are searching for."

So Itchy, Matty and Norm set about finding suitable wood to make their craft – no easy task with it being damp and without twigs large enough to be of any use.

For two days the trio gathered branches, placing them in a neat pile so they could choose the best pieces for their raft. Eventually, Itchy started to lay them out on the ground in a line, selecting branches of equal length and roughly the same thickness.

Making the raft

Norm and Matty hunted for pieces of ivy and creeper to tie them together until finally, the raft was taking shape. All they needed now was a sail.

"I know," Norm offered kindly, "we could use my red handkerchief. If we have one branch tied upright we could fasten the handkerchief to it as our sail. Then as the wind catches it we could pick up quite a speed. We will be there in no time." Norm folded the scarf into a triangular shape and tied it fast to the centre pole.

With the raft completed, its red sail blowing in the autumn wind, the three of them carefully pushed it into the river and climbed aboard nervously as it swayed from side to side in the cold water. The craft rocked perilously on the waves, leaving the three of them to hang on tightly to the mast as they tried to keep their balance while clinging on to their food supplies.

The raft was buffeted from side to side as it made its way downstream, being pulled along swiftly by the torrent of grey raging water that seemed to be trying to tip them out. But they clung on tightly, the wind whistling in their ears and their fur blowing in all directions. Matty resembled a matted rug; it would take some grooming to restore her coat to any sort of normality.

The river was noisy as well as fast, so conversation between them was not easy. Their eyes were so tightly shut that they didn't see the geese on the far shore flapping their wings to warn them of dangers that lay ahead.

In front of them, some fifty-upples wide or so, was a weir with a drop of about two upples in length. The river then rushed on, with boulders hidden below that could have smashed the raft to pieces. Itchy, Norm and Matty clung tightly to the wooden structure.

The geese warning the travellers on the raft

"Stop, stop, stop!" cried the geese. But Itchy and his friends were oblivious to any danger, still rushing headlong towards the weir. "Stop, stop!" they cried once more, but it was too late ... The raft tipped over the top of the weir, sending Itchy, Matty and Norm flying through the air and into the rough, cold water. Their paws splayed in all directions, their plight catching them all by surprise!

Itchy and Norm managed to grab at the red sail and hang on to the fabric. With the wind inside, it acted like a parachute. Matty, however, was nowhere to be seen.

The boulders on the riverbed slowed the water a little, the two friends managing to cling on to the red handkerchief and what remained of their raft. Finally, the torrent of water eased and they landed at the side of the riverbank. First thing was to find out what had become of Matty.

Matty had been thrown through the air. Being of a lighter weight than Itchy, she had easily lost her grip on the raft and before she knew it, she found herself splashing about in the river. Time and again she seemed to go underwater, swallowing great mouthfuls of muddy liquid as she did so. Matty thought she might die, as she couldn't swim very well. Then, suddenly, she could feel her fur being tugged at. Something or someone had caught hold of her matted coat and she seemed to be torn upwards.

Up an up she went, seemingly flying – not a feeling a badger is used to. Matty glanced sideways and out of the corner of her eye, she could see that she was being carried by the geese! Two on each side had hold of tufts of her fur and she was being carried towards the riverbank. Placing her gently down, the geese spread their wings to dry them out.

Matty being rescued from the river

"Are you ok?" asked the first goose.

"You gave us quite a fright, you know," said the second goose. "Lucky we are strong."

"That's why we have this job," joined in one of the others, puffing out his chest.

Matty, wet from her fall in the river

"We are the geese lifeguards for this stretch of the river," said goose number one, who was bigger than the others and obviously the head lifeguard. "This stretch of river is very dangerous and claimed several lives until we formed our team." He spread out his wings wide to remove the moisture, obviously proud of his role.

"We tried to warn you," said one of the geese, "but you were travelling so fast."

"I'm fine," said Matty. "I'm just wet and my coat is a mess. It will take me ages to groom myself. Have you seen Itchy and Norm? I'm worried about them."

"They are further down the river than us," said one of the geese. "They hung on to the sail and were pushed onto the reeds at the side of the bank. We will escort you to them."

The geese formed a line and introduced themselves to Matty, each one tipping their wing in salute as they said their name.

"I'm Gary," said one of them, followed in turn by Gerald, Godfrey and Gabriel.

"All present and correct," another said, preening his feathers. "I do love a happy ending."

The geese introducing themselves to Matty

"My name is Gordon and I'm the head lifeguard," said the first goose.

"I'm Graham," said the second.

With all the geese accounted for and Matty's fur now drying out, they all made their way in formation towards Itchy and Norm, who were waiting downstream.

The night air was cold and the geese all huddled together for warmth as Itchy, Matty and Norm explained why they were on their journey and what they were looking for.

"So you see," Matty said, gulping back tears, "we must continue our journey or our friends' homes will be destroyed and Badger Wood will be gone forever. No more foraging for berries and fruit. No more night-time trips. And our sett will go, too. We will be forced to find a new home."

The geese gaggled amongst themselves, sympathising with the group but not really having any answers for them.

The next day, cold and dull as it was, the geese decided they would take it in turns to fly over the surrounding area to see if they could see anything of interest from the sky. That way, a lot of ground could be covered quickly and it would give Itchy, Norm and Matty time to rest and recover.

They set off two at a time, the winter morning sun struggling to appear through the pale mist which hung over the river at this time of year. In relays, the geese circled the sky before disappearing from view as they widened their search. One by one, they returned to base to report what they had found.

Graham Goose had seen a farmer digging, Gary had seen some upples with strange things on sticks making a bleeping sound over a green field and Gordon had been to some building sites.

"I know what the stick things are!" cried Norm excitedly. "I think they are metal detectors! The upples sometimes find buried treasure with those. I think we ought to take a look for ourselves."

Upples with metal detectors

There was great excitement amongst the group as they wondered what on earth could be buried in the field. Had they found anything yet? they wondered. And could it be of any value? Could they take it home and save their wood, after all?

Waving their new friends goodbye, Itchy, Norm and Matty left for the field clutching a bag with nuts, seeds and leftover bread that the geese had kindly given them. Gary flew overhead to lead the way and then when the upples were in sight, he tipped his wings from side to side then disappeared into the cloudy sky.

Faced with all these upples, the trio felt nervous. They had never been up this close to the enemy before. It was strange to watch them shouting then bending their ear towards the ground to listen to the bleeping sounds coming from their machines. The open countryside was surrounded by bushes, so Matty suggested they hide and wait until darkness fell. The upples would have gone home by then and it would be safe to enter the field.

It had started to rain by the time the upples had left and the heavy shower had made the grass underfoot a quagmire. Itchy looked over his shoulder nervously in case someone had stayed behind before cautiously entering the field. He was closely followed by Matty and Norm and together, they crept into the middle of the field, keeping low as they did so. They were wary on unfamiliar ground.

"Can you see anything?" asked Matty.

The rain was becoming heavier now and the field was pitch-black, the moon hidden behind the clouds.

Norm said, "I wish we were tucked up somewhere warm, preferably with a nice slice of pizza. I don't mean to sound ungrateful, but I'm not overkeen on seeds or worms and I don't like the dark, either."

"It's the mud I don't like," Matty replied. "I've only just groomed myself after falling in the river."

The three of them began to search the field, moving slowly up and down in lines methodically.

Hours later they still hadn't found anything and they began to lose heart. Maybe there was nothing here, after all, thought Itchy. This could be a wild goose chase.

Itchy, Matty and Norm searching the field

Itchy, Matty and Norm were tired and soaking wet, their spirits low. Hungry as well now, they retreated to the cover of the hedgerow to search for worms and get some sleep.

Daylight gradually gave way to a damp, still evening, the greyness of the weather reflecting their mood.

"What are we going to do now?" Norm said, voicing what they had all been thinking but had been afraid to put into words.

"I don't know," said Itchy. "Something will turn up; it has to. Either that or we are all in trouble. The rest of our woodland friends are relying on us; we can't let them down."

The friends sheltered under the hedgerow throughout the next day, emerging only at night. They made their way further along the edge of the field, then across a muddy, ploughed area, getting dangerously near to a housing estate. Suddenly, Norm stopped in his tracks, his whiskers twitching. He could smell something.

"Oooh! what's that lovely smell?" he gasped, leaning towards the scent as it wafted towards him on the night air.

"I don't know," Matty replied. "I can smell something."

"I think it's cheese," said Itchy.

Norm, unable to help himself, began to walk in a trance-like state, his eyes almost closed, towards the wonderful aroma.

"I think it's pizza!" he called out excitedly. "Look out, pizza, here I come!"

As he began to move faster, Itchy and Matty grabbed hold of his tail to try to slow him down.

"No! No!" said Itchy. "I think the smell is coming from one of the upples's homes. You can't just go in there. You're much bigger than a normal mouse and they will see you!"

Norm was not happy. The smell of pizza beckoned him. But he could understand the danger Itchy thought they were in. Not wanting to get caught, they progressed more slowly on tiptoe towards the end of the garden.

The garden was laid out mainly to grass, with a path running down the length of it.

On one side there appeared to be a vegetable patch, now dismal owing to the cold weather, weeds wet and sodden underfoot. On the other side a children's slide and a swing belonging to the upples lay abandoned, toys scattered around, forgotten. A light shining through the gap in the curtains from the dining room let a chink of light into the garden. As the friends kept low, a woman emerged from the back door and scraped the remnants of a pizza into the bin.

"It *is* pizza!" Norm whispered excitedly. "I'd know that smell anywhere, and she's throwing it away!"

"We still need to be careful," advised Itchy as he scratched his thigh. "We need to wait to make sure no one comes out again."

They waited patiently until all the lights in the house had gone out and they were quite sure the upples were in bed before they made their way gingerly up the path towards the back door.

Norm was so excited he could hardly contain himself. The thought of his favourite food after weeks of worms and berries was almost too much to bear. He flipped open the lid of the bin and dived in head-first.

He scattered rubbish all over the grass, grinning all over his face. He couldn't believe his luck. Rummaging around in the bin, Norm found himself momentarily stuck upside down, until Itchy and Matty grabbed his hind legs to pull him out. Triumphantly, he held up a portion of pizza and the remains of some still in the box, cheese and tomato sticking to his whiskers as he spoke.

"Oh, will you look at this," Norm declared. "I knew it smelt delicious, come and try some!"

"Thank you, but no. While you were upside down we were snuffling around in the grass," declared Itchy, "and Matty has found some bulbs, so that will do us fine."

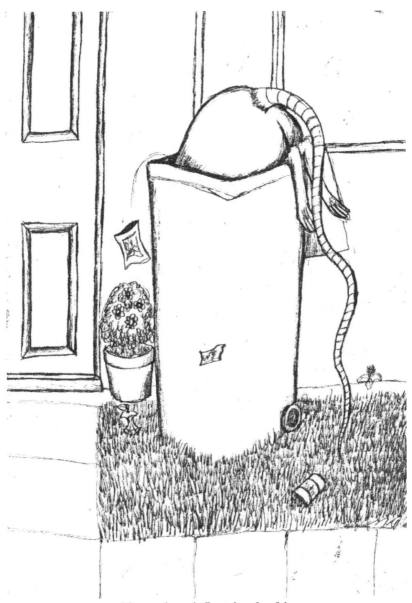

Norm head-first in the bin

The three of them sat in the moonlit garden enjoying their feast noisily and relaxing. Suddenly, they heard noises coming from inside the house. The back door was flung wide open and an upple appeared in the kitchen doorway in her nightdress and slippers, shaking a rolling pin in her hand, shouting.

"Get out of my garden! How dare you dig up my grass! Get out! Get out!"

Itchy, Matty and Norm tore up the path as fast as they could as all manner of things were hurled after them.

"I don't think she wants to teach us how to cook!" Matty laughed as she ducked to avoid a flying plate, narrowly missing her head.

They hurried to the shelter of the hedgerow and trees nearby, still clutching their food, not wanting to go hungry after all that excitement.

The trio running from an angry upple

A couple of days later, Itchy, Matty and Norm made their way along a muddy trail, wondering where to go next. Eventually, they saw a badger in the distance, hurrying along, and decided to follow him to see if he'd heard of anything of value being found locally that they could use to save their wood.

The trio had to run to catch up with him as he was quite a way away and moving at rather a pace. They were surprised when he disappeared from view only to reappear some 15 upples in height away.

"Hey," called Itchy. "Wait for us; we need some help."

The badger turned and looked in their direction, his coat almost blending in to the once lush green surroundings, now limp and dull in the damp winter air. The only sign that indicated he was near a sett were the mounds of earth and piles of leaves around him.

The badger looking over his shoulder at Itchy

"What is it?" called out the badger crossly in irritation at being held up. "I have to get home; I think it's going to snow."

"We thought so, too," said Matty. "It's so cold and we are far away from our sett, but we are on a journey to save our wood and wondered if you could help."

"Follow me," answered the badger. "It's too cold to chat out here and we have plenty of room. You can tell me all about it then."

The badger's sett was huge, bigger than Itchy and Matty had ever seen. There must have been at least ten entrances. From outside it just looked like a pile of leaves and earth, but inside small, neat doors were in place.

Once inside, the friends looked around in wonder at the scene that greeted them. It was well lit and the rooms were high, taller than those at Itchy and Matty's home. Open-plan rooms led off one another with corridors linking all the spaces. This was how the badger had disappeared only to resurface elsewhere.

There were several badgers all involved in different tasks. Some were cleaning, others cooking and still others arriving with worms, mushrooms and bugs. A whole industry, it seemed, all busy foraging for whatever foodstuff they could find while the ground was still fairly soft in places, as soon it would be frozen solid.

The badgers cooking

"My name is Scurry," declared the badger. "We have heard about your journey. News travels fast in these parts. The entire countryside is buzzing." He sighed, shaking his head slowly from side to side. "Very sad news, but how can we help you? I have no idea."

"Do you know of anywhere that we might be able to find old things?" asked Itchy. "Something we could distract the upples with."

Matty joined in. "We need to save the woodland and if we put something old in the ground, the upples might go away."

"We could ask Auntie Twiddle," pondered Scurry, scratching. "She knows a lot of things and is very wise."

"Auntie Twiddle!" squealed Itchy and Matty together. "*Our* Auntie Twiddle?"

"Well I don't know if she's your Auntie Twiddle," replied Scurry. "She has lived here for a long time now but I don't know where she lived before."

Scurry led them through a long corridor with large rooms at the end. It almost seemed to be separate from the others and was luxuriously furnished. Itchy, Matty and Norm had never seen anything like it before.

There, in front of a huge roaring fire, covered in a thick red blanket, sat an old badger, her fur now greying all over. It was dull and it had lost its once youthful sheen. It was *their* Auntie Twiddle.

"How did you get here?" gasped Itchy.

Auntie Twiddle was partially deaf, so Itchy had to get up close so she could hear him.

"Well, well, well," whispered Auntie Twiddle, her eyebrows so thick they almost covered her eyes. She had to squint to see everybody and she peered at Itchy. "It's Itchy, isn't it? And who are these other fine creatures?"

Itchy introduced Matty and Norm then explained how they came to be in the area. What they all really wanted to know, though, was how Auntie Twiddle had come to be so far away from her home. What had happened to her?

Auntie Twiddle telling the story of how she went missing

"I went out one night searching for food. You are probably too young to remember, but the weather was cold, colder than it had been for a long time." She sighed and moved her fur with a long claw.

"Go on," said Itchy, struggling to make out the tired old badger's words.

Auntie Twiddle caught in the badger trap

"I walked for miles searching and searching, looking for something nice to cook, but the ground was really hard and food was in short supply. Anyway ..." Auntie Twiddle paused and sighed once more. "I went out of my normal area but got caught in a badger trap. I was caught fast and couldn't escape.

"I really thought that was the end for me. I called and called for help and then I saw upples coming towards me."

"What did you do?" gasped Itchy.

Auntie Twiddle smiling after telling her story

"Nothing I could do," continued Auntie Twiddle. "But would you believe, there are some nice ones about. They took me to a hospital to be checked over. Luckily I wasn't badly hurt, just shocked. And then he brought me here. You are now in Badgerworld."

"So that's where we are," laughed Itchy. "But we can't bring our woodland friends here and we really would prefer to go back to our home in Badger Wood."

"Back to your problem of how to save your wood. I have heard about something which may be of help to you," whispered the old badger. "It's a place called Rainbow Ravine. Badgers used to say if you could get to the end of the rainbow, right at the very end of the beam of light, you will find a pot of golden treasures. More than enough to solve all your problems."

The trio looked at each other in utter amazement. They had never heard of such a story.

"So in what direction does this Rainbow Ravine lie?" asked Itchy.

Norm was worried about the weather. They had such a lot of rain recently and the ground underfoot was very wet. Not to mention the imminent threat of snow. He certainly didn't fancy trekking very far.

"Ahhh!" said Auntie. "That's the best part." She smiled, showing her yellowing badger teeth. "When it rains at this time of year and then the sun breaks through the clouds, that is when the best and brightest of rainbows appear. All you need to do is follow it to the end. You need to move fast, as the rainbow doesn't last long. You need to be at the end to find the treasure before it vanishes."

Itchy clapped his hands together in excitement and looked at Matty and Norm. Delight edged across his badger brow, his eyes sparkling.

"This has to be it!" he exclaimed. "We set off tomorrow."

At dusk the three friends gathered food together that the other badgers had collected before saying their goodbyes and starting out on their journey.

They travelled on for several nights, sheltering from the cool day air under hedgerows and trees, living on berries and worms. Once or twice they spotted the faint glow of a rainbow in the distance, but each time it faded to a shimmering light, which disappeared as they neared it.

On the fifth day they were beginning to despair of ever finding it, when Matty had an idea.

"I don't think rainbows happen much at night," she said. "I know we don't like it much, but I think we have to search for one during the day."

"There are extra risks involved," answered Itchy doubtfully. "For a start, we have to keep an eye out for upples. They are still culling badgers and will shoot us if they have a chance."

Hiding from upples while searching for the rainbow

"And," joined in Norm, "we will need to stay well away from roads. The traffic is terrible during daylight hours. We don't want to get run over."

Eventually, after much discussion, the three agreed to give the daytime a chance.

With the damp grey drizzle hanging heavy in the air and only the sound of starlings gathering overhead, the friends, now cold and weary, started to look for their rainbow. In one long line, with no one saying very much, they stuck to the edges of fields, staying well away from roads and houses. All day they trudged onwards through the mud, almost giving up hope, when suddenly Itchy cried, "Look! Look!"

Matty and Norm lifted their tired heads to see what Itchy was shouting about and pointing at.

"*Look!*" he shouted louder, and there, right before them, was the most magnificent and brightly coloured rainbow any of them had ever seen.

The friends find the rainbow

An enormous arc of colours lit up the early evening sky. Red, orange, yellow, green, blue, indigo and violet all in bands. They shone brightly, the end of which seemed to disappear over the edge of a ravine.

"Quick!" yelled Matty, "we need to get to the end before it vanishes!"

"Run!" shouted Itchy.

The three friends ran as fast as their little legs would carry them towards the edge of the light. But to their dismay, the light did indeed appear to disappear over the edge of the ravine, so how could they get down to the start of it?

Norm once again came to the rescue. He quickly unfurled his massive long tail and threw it down the side of the ravine, being careful not to let its weight topple him over the edge.

"Come on!" he shouted urgently to Itchy and Matty. "Slide down my tail and you can get down to the treasure!"

"How will you get down, though?" panted Matty, concern etched across her badger face. Her fur stood up more than normal and her black eyes sparkled with tears at the kindness of their friend and the thought of leaving him behind.

"Don't worry about me, just hurry!" said Norm. "I will think of something – we haven't time to hesitate or the rainbow will be gone!"

Itchy decided to go first. "It looks quite a drop, but I'll give it a go," he said bravely. "If you think your tail is long enough?"

Gripping Norm's tail with his front paws and trying not to scratch his tail too much, Itchy began to slide downwards.

"Wheee ..." he shouted as he gathered speed, beginning to enjoy himself. "It's easy!" he called up to Matty as he dropped the last few upples in height onto the muddy soil. "Your turn, Matty. It's not far and it's lovely and warm down here."

Matty cautiously climbed onto Norm's tail, closed her eyes and slid down to join Itchy.

Norm, not wanting to be left out of all the excitement, decided to slide down the mud on his ample bottom. "Oh! Oh! Oh!" he cried as he bounced his way over boulders. He hit stones on the way, bouncing from side to side until he landed with a thud at Itchy's feet.

Itchy sliding down Norm's tail into the ravine

The three friends looked at each other in surprise. They had done it! They were at the base of the rainbow ...

Itchy looked at Matty to see if she was all right and his eyes widened as he said, "You look all yellow! Are you ok?"

"I'm fine," Matty replied, "but you look all blue!"

They both looked at Norm. "You're green!" they echoed together and with that, they all fell about in fits of laughter as they took turns to dance in different coloured lights emanating from the rainbow.

Once they had recovered and reminded each other why they were there, they began to dig at the damp mud where the light was coming out of the ground.

"Quickly! Quickly!" Itchy urged his friends; he was worried the rainbow would disappear before they found the gold. If Auntie Twiddle was right, this could be just the treasure they needed to save Badger Wood.

The three of them scrambled at the earth, digging wildly, and then Itchy shouted.

"My claw touched something! There is something here! Help me dig it up and lift it out."

They all shoved their claws beneath the muddy lump. To their amazement, they had found a golden pot. Wiping it clean as best they could, the pot shone in the fading light. It had four small feet on the base. But best of all, it was filled to the brim with golden coins and other smaller pots which gleamed.

"Oh Itchy!" exclaimed Matty. "We've done it!" She looked at Itchy, her eyes sparkling with tears of happiness.

Norm and Itchy appeared to be in a daze as they gazed at the treasure they had just dug up, scarcely able to believe their eyes.

The light began to fade and the rainbow vanished into the damp evening air, leaving the three of them wondering what to do next. How on earth were they going to get out?

Itchy, Matty and Norm find the pot of gold

Norm was down there with them, so they couldn't use his tail to climb out, and the pot was quite stuck in the mud at the foot of the ravine.

As everyone knows, the pot of gold stays at the end of the rainbow and is refilled whenever the rainbow shines again. But would they be able to move enough of the treasure to save Badger Wood? And could they get back home in time before the upples came?

Suddenly, Itchy thought he could hear upples voices coming from just above their heads, which was bound to signal danger.

What happened next was absolutely amazing ...

The Brave and Adventurous Tales of Itchybald Scratchet

Itchybald Scratchet (Itchy) is a badger who lives quietly with his wife, Matty, in a sett (a badger's home) in Badger Wood.

While out one day foraging for winter food, he goes further away from his sett than normal. On his way home he bumps into a pheasant, who informs him that their home in Badger Wood is about to be built on for housing the upples (badger name for people).

Distracted and upset by this news, Itchy falls into a disused well on his way home. Trapped and alone, he is eventually rescued by a large mouse called Enor or Norm, who becomes his friend.

After discussing the house-building plans with the rest of the woodland animals Itchy, Matty and Norm set out on an adventure to save their homes so Badger Wood won't be built on. The long and dangerous journey takes them in search of treasure in the fields around the wood, but they are helped on their way. To their delight they find a long-lost Aunt, who tells them the secret of how to save their homes. When they reach their destination, they find themselves trapped. After hearing upples voices above them, Itchy and his friends have to get away without being seen.

What happens next is amazing ... Find out how they save Badger Wood in the second book of the series:

Itchybald Scratchet – Return from Rainbow Ravine

Badger Wood